The average child in America will wear down 730 **crayons** by his or her tenth birthday.

AaBb Cc

A **rabbit**'s teeth never stop growing.

More than 450,000 **school buses** transport close to 24 million students in the U.S. to school every school day.

To the first day of school and
the beginning of a great adventure
—P.S.

For Jane, Owen, Sophia, and Andrew
and the teachers who will teach them,
and for Ingrid
—S.H.

I Love School!
Text copyright © 2004 by Philemon Sturges
Illustrations copyright © 2004 by Shari Halpern
Printed in the U.S.A.   All rights reserved.   www.harperchildrens.com

Library of Congress Cataloging-in-Publication Data   Sturges, Philemon.
I love school! / by Philemon Sturges ; illustrated by Shari Halpern.   p.   cm.
Summary: A brother and sister describe the things they love to do
during their day at kindergarten.
ISBN 0-06-009284-X — ISBN 0-06-009285-8 (lib. bdg.)
[1. Kindergarten—Fiction. 2. Schools—Fiction. 3. Brothers and sisters—Fiction.
4. Stories in rhyme.] I. Halpern, Shari, ill. II. Title.
PZ8.3.S9227 Iad 2004 2002068554
[E]—dc21 CIP AC

1 2 3 4 5 6 7 8 9 10
❖
First Edition

I Love School !

BY **Philemon Sturges**

ILLUSTRATED BY **Shari Halpern**

HarperCollins Publishers

School, school, school,
I love school!

I love the bus that comes this way,
To take us where we'll spend the day.
With all my friends I laugh and sing.
I talk about most everything.

I love to build great big block walls.

I love to play with baby dolls.

I like to draw trains speeding by.

I like to paint birds flying high.

It's recess when the school bell rings!
I like the slides.

I like the swings.

I kick the ball when we go out.

I just like to run and shout.

I count numbers—1, 2, 3.

I write letters—X, Y, Z!

Let's watch Harvey Rabbit munch.

I can hardly wait for lunch!

I'll trade my yummy cheese and ham
For your peanut butter–jam.

Won't do that, but I will trade
My apple juice for lemonade!

It's story time. Let's read the book
About a trip some sailors took
To a strange land far away.
Perhaps we'll go there too someday!

And what I like the most . . .
You guessed . . .

Is our teacher—
She's the best!

School, school, school,
I love school!

A **pencil** will write in zero gravity, upside down, and underwater.

Lunch box: In the 1930s, toy makers began selling tin pails and boxes for carrying lunch.

The world's largest **peanut-butter-and-jelly sandwich** contained 150 pounds of peanuts and 50 pounds of jelly.

CAT